THE ZACK FILES ™

This Body's Not Big Enough for Both of Us

LETTERS TO DAN GREENBURG
ABOUT THE ZACK FILES:

From a mother in New York, NY: "Just wanted to let you know that it was THE ZACK FILES that made my son discover the joy of reading...I tried everything to get him interested...THE ZACK FILES turned my son into a reader overnight. Now he complains when he's out of books!"

From a boy named Toby in New York, NY: "The reason why I like your books is because you explain things that no other writer would even dream of explaining to kids."

From Tara in Floral Park, NY: "When I read your books I felt like I was in the book with you. We love your books!"

From a teacher in West Chester, PA: "I cannot thank you enough for writing such a fantastic series."

From Max in Old Bridge, NJ: "I wasn't such a great reader until I discovered your books."

From Monica in Burbank, IL: "I read almost all of your books and I loved the ones I read. I'm a big fan! *I'm Out of My Body, Please Leave a Message*. That's a funny title. It makes me think of it being the best book in the world."

From three mothers in Toronto: "You have managed to take three boys and unlock the world of reading. In January they could best be characterized as boys who 'read only under duress.' Now these same guys are similar in that they are motivated to READ."

From Stephanie in Hastings, NY: "If someone didn't like your books that would be crazy."

From Dana in Floral Park, NY: "I really LOVE I mean LOVE your books. I read them a million times. I wish I could buy more. They are so good and so funny."

From a teacher in Pelham, NH: "My students are thoroughly enjoying [THE ZACK FILES]. Some are reading a book a night."

From Madeleine in Hastings, NY: "I love your books...I hope you keep making many more Zack Files."

THE ZACK FILES ™

This Body's Not Big Enough for Both of Us

By Dan Greenburg

Illustrated by Jack E. Davis

GROSSET & DUNLAP • NEW YORK

For Judith, and for the real Zack,
with love—D.G.

I'd like to thank my editor
Jane O'Connor, who makes the process
of writing and revising so much fun,
and without whom
these books would not exist.

I also want to thank Jill Jarnow,
Emily Sollinger, Monique Stephens
and Tui Sutherland for their terrific ideas.

Library of Congress Cataloging-in-Publication Data is available.

ISBN 0-448-42176-3   E F G H I J

Chapter 1

Have you ever known somebody who was really annoying but you just couldn't get rid of them? That's the way I felt about this old lady I met. Probably her being dead made her even more annoying. Oh, did I mention she was a ghost? Well, she was.

I guess I should begin at the beginning.

My name is Zack. I'm ten and a half and I go to the Horace Hyde-White School for Boys. That's in New York City. Ever since my parents got divorced, I've lived half of the time with my dad. He's a freelance writer, which means he gets to work at home a lot.

The time I want to tell you about started when Dad was writing this article about the new Madame Chateau's Wax Museum. There's been a Madame Chateau's Wax Museum in London for years. In it are wax dummies of famous people both dead and alive. And they look amazingly lifelike. At least that's what people say. The new Madame Chateau's is in Times Square. Dad took me there one Friday evening for a special preview for reporters and VIPs. I was pretty excited.

The night we went, they were holding a séance as a publicity stunt. A séance is when a bunch of people get together in a dark room and try to get a ghost to talk to them. Before the séance got started, Dad and I looked around the museum. There were wax dummies of just about every

famous person who ever lived. Kings, queens, generals, baseball players, movie stars, murderers—you name it. Not all of the dummies were finished. Some of the kings and queens were still without heads. But most of them were done. They stood in the dim light, staring out at you. They looked so real it was spooky.

The séance was being held in a small theater in the museum. On the stage in the theater was a long table with a bunch of people sitting down around it. I guess we were the last to arrive.

"Ah, *there* you are, my dears!" called a lady at the table. She wore a big turban with ostrich feathers sticking out of it, and a jacket with lots of beads on it. "We were beginning to fear that something *dreadful* had happened to you!"

"Sorry we're late," said Dad.

"Well, come up on stage and let's get

started!" called the lady with the turban. "The dead are dying to speak to us!"

I giggled. I thought she was kidding, but she wasn't smiling. Neither were the other people at the table. There were four of them besides the turban lady. There was a guy with a bushy white beard, and two ladies with white hair and very pink cheeks. There was a man with pasty-looking, yellowish skin who looked kind of dead himself. Not that I've ever seen dead people.

"I want the young man to sit next to me," said the feathered lady, smiling at me.

I shrugged and sat down next to her. I don't usually like to sit next to ladies who wear turbans and feathers. But I was too polite to refuse.

"Hi," I said. "I'm Zack."

"And I, of course, am the famous Madam Poopah."

Madam Poopah held out her hand to me,

but it was bent down at the wrist so it was hard to shake. Sometimes, in movies, queens do that. You're supposed to kiss their hand. I wasn't about to kiss anything. I grabbed her wrist and shook it. Her skin was ice-cold.

On the table was a crystal ball and a huge wax candle.

"Are you ready to speak with the dead?" she asked me. She was smiling, but I could tell she was serious.

"I guess so," I said.

"I'll bet you've never spoken to the dead before," said the pasty-looking guy. He had kind of a fake smile on his face.

"I guess not," I said.

"What about Wanda?" said Dad.

"Oh, right," I answered. "Once this really bratty poltergeist trashed my dad's apartment. She talked to me. Her name was Wanda."

"Poltergeists don't talk," said the pasty-looking guy.

"This one did," I said. "Not with a voice. She spelled out messages on the ceiling with peanut M&Ms."

"He's telling the truth," said Dad. "I was there."

"How marvelous!" said one of the white-haired ladies. "But why peanut M&M's?"

"We were out of the plain ones," I said.

"All right," said Madam Poopah. "Now let us begin."

She nodded and closed her eyes. The lights in the theater got very dim and then went out. The crystal ball started glowing. I don't know how she did that.

"Let us all join hands," said Madam Poopah softly to us. "Join hands and clear our minds."

Dad took one of my hands, and Madam Poopah took the other. Her hand was cold as a frozen TV dinner. That really creeped me out. Also, she smelled like garlic.

"This is Madam Poopah," she said in a louder voice. "We are calling to spirits on the other side. Is there anyone on the other side who would like to speak to us?"

There was no answer. I was pretty sure that what she meant by "the other side" wasn't Russia. It meant the spirit world.

"Anyone at all on the other side who would like to chat," she said. "please, come forward, my dears, and make yourselves known to us."

There still was no answer.

"We are here, seven of us, eager to speak to the spirits of the departed," said Madam Poopah. "Anyone at all who cares to speak to us, please give us some sign."

"Maybe they're all at a movie or something," I said.

Everybody but Dad gave me a dirty look.

"Ssshhh!" said Madam Poopah. "Sometimes it takes them a while to get through to us. It's quite difficult for the dead to communicate with the living."

There still was no answer.

Then I heard a weird high-pitched noise. It was coming from Madam Poopah. I wanted her to stop, but I was afraid to tell her.

Then something even weirder happened. I felt a kind of tingling from Madam Poopah's hand. Then something that felt like a slight electric shock. It reminded me of the time I accidentally electrocuted myself in science class and started reading minds.

Then I heard a ghostly voice.

"Who dares to disturb the spirits of the dead?" it said.

It was the voice of a very grouchy old lady. It had a strong British accent.

But the weirdest thing about the voice was...it was coming from *me!*

Chapter 2

"**Z**ack, is that you?" whispered my dad. "Please, don't horse around anymore, son. The people here are very serious about this séance."

"Dad," I whispered, "I'm not horsing around." And then, without even knowing I was going to do it, I said in this grouchy British old lady voice: **"And we shall thank you not to speak to us unless spoken to."**

"I mean it, Zack," said Dad. "This is no joke. These people are here to try to communicate with the dead. And I'm going to write about it. If you keep horsing around like this, we'll both have to leave."

I sighed. "Dad, I *swear* to you, I'm not horsing around," I said. "I don't know what's happening. But it's nothing I'm doing—honest!"

"He's telling the truth," said Madam Poopah. "It *isn't* something Zack is doing. At least, not on purpose."

"But the voice of that grouchy old British gal came from Zack," said Dad. "I know. I'm sitting right next to him."

"That grouchy old British gal?" I said—or, somebody *inside* me said. **"That grouchy old British gal? You dare to speak of Her Highness as 'that grouchy old British gal?'"**

Voices coming from inside of me? This was really freaking me out. How could this be happening?

"I think I know what's happening

here," said the guy with the bushy white beard. "A spirit of the departed has chosen Zack. It will speak through Zack. This is wonderful!"

"Your son must be very psychic," said Madam Poopah to my dad. She turned to me. "Are you psychic, my dear?"

"No," I said. "But I *did* read minds one day in science class, after I almost got electrocuted. And there was another time I talked to dolphins by ESP."

"Then that's it!" Madam Poopah told Dad. "Your son has the gift! He's channeling a spirit from the other side! Usually that sort of thing happens to *me*. But for some reason it's happening to Zack instead. This is a great honor! Zack, do you realize what a great honor this is?"

"Cease this infernal racket," said the voice inside of me.

"Who is speaking through Zack?" asked

Madam Poopah in a creepy voice. "Please, spirit, tell us your name."

"The Queen does not answer questions," I said in the weird British voice. The way I said "answer" made it sound like "on-sir."

"Pardon me, Your Highness," said Madam Poopah. "I did not mean to offend you. Pray, tell me. Which queen am I speaking to?"

"*Which* queen? *Which* queen? We are *Victoria*, you nincompoop."

"Queen Victoria of England!" said the guy with the bushy white beard. "Hey, this is great! I've never met her before."

"This is indeed an honor, Queen Victoria," said Madam Poopah. "What can we do for you, Your Majesty?"

"What can you do for us? You can take us to the bloody W.C. That's what you can do for us."

"The what?" I asked in my normal voice.

"W.C. means water closet," Madam Poopah whispered. "In England, the water closet means the toilet. Zack, she wants you to take her to the bathroom."

"But I don't have to go," I said, a little embarrassed.

"Well, maybe *she* does," said one of the white-haired ladies. "Say, maybe *I* could take her. I'd like to visit the rest room myself."

"How could *you* take her, Mildred?" asked the other white-haired lady. "The queen is inside of *Zack*, not you."

"Good point," said Mildred.

"We do not care who takes us," I said in the queen's voice. **"But somebody had better take us right now before we have an accident."**

"What's this 'we' business?" I asked again in my normal voice.

"She's speaking in the royal 'we'," explained Madam Poopah. "All kings and queens speak that way. They use 'we' instead of 'I.'"

"Are we going to the bloody W.C., or are we going to have an accident?" I shouted.

"Dad, what should I do?" I whispered in my normal voice.

"Um, I guess you'd better take her to the bloody W.C.," said Dad.

Chapter 3

Once I got down off the stage and out into lobby, the rest rooms were right down-stairs. I trotted downstairs and pushed open the door of the men's room. A man about my dad's age was drying his hands at the hot air blower.

"What *is* this place?" I shouted in the queen's voice.

The man looked at me, startled.

"It's the men's rest room," said the man. "What did you *think* it was?"

"*I* know it's the men's rest room," I

said. "It wasn't me who asked you. It was this queen of England inside me named Victoria."

The man stopped drying his hands and slipped quietly out the door.

"This is not a proper W.C. This is a men's rest room. Why have you taken us to a *men's* rest room?"

"Because I'm a guy, Your Highness," I said.

"Take us to a *ladies'* rest room."

"But I'm not a lady, Your Highness," I said. "I can't go in there."

Another man walked inside and headed toward the urinals.

"Do it! Do it *now*," I said in the queen's voice.

The man looked nervously in my direction.

"I will not go to the ladies' rest room," I said under my breath. "And that's for sure."

**"Go to the ladies' rest room immedi-
ately, and that's a royal *command*."**

Being careful not to look in my direction,
the man walked quickly out of the room.

"Well, I'm a citizen of the United States
of America," I said. "And I don't take
commands from anybody but the president
and my dad!"

"We shall see about that."

And then, even though I'd just about
decided I had to go to the bathroom after
all, I felt my legs start walking me out of the
room.

"Hey!" I said. "What are you doing?"

I tried to head back toward the urinals,
but my legs wouldn't let me. I smacked my
head into the door on the way out.

"Stop this!" I said. "I don't care if you're
a queen, I am not taking orders from you!"

My legs carried me through the lobby
to the ladies' room.

"No way am I going to the ladies' room," I said. "No way am I going through that door!"

My legs headed right for the door of the ladies' room. Just before they carried me through it, I reached out and grabbed the doorway on each side with both hands and hung on tight.

"Let go. Let go of this doorway immediately."

"No way!" I said.

A stuffy-looking lady walked up to me. She was some kind of museum guard.

"And what, may I ask, are *you* doing, young man?" she asked me.

"Trying not to go into the ladies' room," I said.

"I beg your pardon?" said the lady.

"I'm trying not to go in here. I don't want to go into the ladies' room."

"Well, I should *hope* not," she said.

"This is too tiresome," I said in the queen's voice. **"Return us to the séance immediately. If not sooner."**

I was pretty relieved to hear myself say that.

When I got back to the séance, I got straight to the point.

"Madam Poopah," I said, "I'd really like you to get this queen out of me. She's a royal pain."

"You don't want her?" said Mildred. "Then give her to me."

"No, me," said her friend. "I'd *love* to have Queen Victoria inside of me."

"Ladies, ladies!" said Madam Poopah. "One cannot simply give a spirit away. A spirit is not a bologna sandwich. A spirit decides whom it wishes to inhabit, and when it wishes to leave."

"Then we all want spirits of our own, like Zack," said the bearded guy.

"Yeah," said the pasty-looking guy. "I want one, too!"

"People, listen to me!" Madam Poopah said. "You think I have spirits in a bag and can just pass them out like lollipops? I do not. Besides, if anyone deserves to have Queen Victoria move into her, it is I. You know, Zack, if I were you, I'd realize what an honor it is to have a member of royalty inside of me. I'd try to get used to her. She won't stay forever, you know. And when she *does* leave, you may wish she hadn't."

Yeah, right.

Chapter 4

When I woke up Saturday morning, I was achy and stiff, like I'd run a marathon the day before. I couldn't stand up straight. I walked bent over like an old man.

"Zack, what's wrong with you?" Dad asked when he saw me. "You're walking like you're about eighty years old."

"Well," I said, **"that's because we *are* eighty years old."**

"OK, that settles it," said Dad. "Zack, I'm taking you and Victoria to Dr. Kropotkin."

Dad made a quick call to the doctor's

office. I have a feeling that Dr. Kropotkin doesn't have all that many patients. He is *always* able to fit us in without an appointment.

We were there in twenty minutes. When Dr. Kropotkin tried to look down my throat and listen to my heart, the queen kept shoving him away. He acted like there was nothing weird about that.

"Well," said Dr. Kropotkin, putting away his stethoscope. "That completes my examination of Zack."

"And what did you find?" Dad asked.

"I find everything absolutely normal..."

"Really?" said Dad.

"...for an eighty year old woman," said Dr. Kropotkin. "And—this is peculiar—I distinctly heard two heartbeats. Why do you suppose that would be?"

"Possibly because I've got Queen Victoria inside of me," I said.

"Oh, then that would definitely explain it," said Dr. Kropotkin. He snapped his clipboard shut. "So, is there anything else?"

Dad and I looked at each other.

"Don't you have any suggestions, Doctor?" Dad asked.

"For what?" said Dr. Kropotkin.

"For getting her out of me," I answered.

"And you'd want to do that because...?"

"Because she's annoying," I said. "She makes me pee in public ladies' rooms. She orders me around. She makes me say these really embarrassing things."

"I haven't heard her say anything," said Dr. Kropotkin.

"Well, you saw her shoving you before. Maybe she's sleeping now," I said. "She takes a lot of naps. I guess because she's so old."

"*Old?* You think us *old?* That really hurts our feelings."

"See what I mean?" I said.

"Hmmm," said Dr. Kropotkin.

"Have you ever seen anything like this?" Dad asked.

"Not so much with queens," said Dr. Kropotkin.

"What can I do?" I asked.

"Drink plenty of fluids, rest in bed, gargle with salt water, and call me in the morning," said Dr. Kropotkin.

"And will that help?"

"I doubt it," said Dr. Kropotkin.

"I think there's only one person who can help us," said Dad. "Madam Poopah."

Chapter 5

Dad got Madam Poopah's address from the guard at Madam Chateau's Wax Museum. Dad said he needed it for the article he was writing. I felt funny about going to her for help, especially on a Saturday. But if anybody knew how to get Queen Victoria out of my body it was the person who got her in there in the first place.

"Well, my dears," said Madam Poopah, opening the door of her apartment. "What a surprise to see you two again."

"Can we come in?" I said.

"Of course, of course," she said. "Come in."

We walked into her apartment. There was weird music playing on her stereo. And there was a weird smell, like burning leaves.

"What's that smell?" I asked. "Is something on fire?"

"That's incense," said Madam Poopah. "It helps me relax."

"Oh. And what about the music?"

"That's sitar music," said Dad. "From India. Do you like it?"

"Uh, I'm not sure," I said. "It sounds a little too spooky for me."

Madam Poopah laughed.

"So, Zack," she said, "how are you feeling today, my dear?"

"Well, I'm not feeling like my old self. In fact, I'm feeling more and more like... **Her Majesty, Queen Victoria. Queen of**

England and Ireland. Empress of India," I finished in the queen's voice.

Madam Poopah raised her eyebrows.

"Also, it is time for high tea, and we have not been offered so much as a scone."

"See?" I said in my normal voice.

"Forgive my rudeness, Your Highness," said Madam Poopah. "I was just about to take high tea with scones myself. May I serve you now?"

"Hmmph. Well, be quick about it," I said in the queen's voice.

"Right away, Your Highness," said Madam Poopah.

She went into the kitchen and came out carrying a silver tray. On it were a teapot, some cups, and something that looked like little pointy rolls.

"What are those pointy things?" I asked.

"Scones," she said. "English people like them with their tea. I do, too. Here."

She poured a cup of hot tea and handed it to me.

"Uh, no thanks," I said. "I'm not too crazy about tea. Thanks just the same."

"Drink it."

"Sheesh," I said. I took the tea, but I didn't drink it.

"Drink it!"

I drank it. I burned my mouth.

"Ouch!" I said.

"That's not how to drink tea. Who taught you how to drink tea?"

"*Nobody* taught me how to drink tea," I said. "I don't *know* how to drink tea. I don't *like* tea."

"*Learn* how to like it. That's a royal order."

"You can't just order somebody to like something."

"Oh, yes, we can."

I looked at Madam Poopah.

"What should I do here?" I asked her.

She shrugged.

"Learn to like tea, I guess," she said.

"Great," I said. "Listen, Madam Poopah, I really need your help. How can I ever get Queen Victoria out of my body?"

"Why don't we ask her? Your Majesty, Zack would like to know when you plan to leave his body."

"We heard him. We may be dead, but we're not deaf."

"Sorry, your Majesty," said Madam Poopah.

"We shall go when we are good and ready to go, and not a minute sooner. Didn't you know it's rude for a host to ask a guest to leave?"

"A guest is somebody you invite," I said.

"Meaning no disrespect, Your Highness, I didn't invite you to stay in my body."

"True. We just dropped in. You do have a point there. But we are not yet ready to leave."

"You know," said Madam Poopah, "spirits usually appear to the living for a reason. You must try to find out what Queen Victoria's reason is for coming here."

"We do not care to reveal our reason yet," I said in the queen's voice. **"But as long as we're here, why don't you show us about? We should like to see the sights."**

"You want to see the sights in my apartment?" said Madam Poopah.

"Not the sights in your apartment, you nincompoop. The sights in New York."

I looked at Madam Poopah.

"I think you'd better show her around New York," she said.

Chapter 6

Have you ever shown an out-of-town guest around your city? It can be lots of fun. But not if they're a cranky, old, dead queen of England.

First of all, Queen Victoria refused to ride on either buses or subways. She said that was for peasants. She demanded to be taken around in cabs. Dad said we didn't have enough money to do that, but she insisted. So Dad and I set off to show her the city.

Then regular cabs weren't good enough for her. She'd heard there were horse-drawn carriages in New York. She wanted to be driven around in one of those. Dad told her they only have horse-drawn carriages in Central Park. She was pretty grumpy about that.

She insisted we take her to see Queens. When we got there, she was pretty disappointed.

"Where *are* they?" she kept asking.

"Where *are* they? Where are *who*?"

"The *queens.*"

"There are no queens in Queens," I said.

"What?"

"Queens is the name of a borough of New York," Dad explained.

"Hmmph."

So we went back to Manhattan.

We took her to some of the great New York department stores.

We took her to the top of the Empire State Building.

"Why do they call it the *Empire* State Building?" she asked. **"This building is not in the British Empire."**

Then she said she missed speaking to royalty and asked to go to White Castle, Burger King, and Dairy Queen. We saw them from the taxi. We told her those were just places to eat hamburgers and ice cream, and she got kind of depressed.

Every fifteen minutes we had to stop for tea. Tea and scones. Tea and crumpets. Tea and tiny sandwiches so small that I could have put six of them into my mouth at once. Which I did. Which Dad did not appreciate.

And after drinking all that tea, we had to go to the water closet a lot, too. I don't even want to *talk* about that.

She wanted to go to the Statue of Liberty and walk upstairs to the torch. By the time we got to Bedloe's Island in New York Harbor, which is where the Statue of Liberty is, I was exhausted. We stood in a long line for about half an hour. At last we got to the head of the line. Just as we were about to go into the statue, a uniformed guard held up his hand.

"That's it, folks," he said. "No more for tonight. We're closing."

There were moans and groans from the people behind us.

"Couldn't you just let in a few more people?" Dad asked him.

"Nope," he said. "We're closing. Come back tomorrow."

"But we've been waiting in line for half an hour," I said.

"Tough, kid," he answered.

"This is an outrage. We demand that you step aside and allow us to enter immediately."

The guard cocked his head and looked at me strangely.

"Excuse me?" he said.

"Listen," I said in my normal voice. "That wasn't me just now. I—"

"Stand aside, young man."

"Get lost, kid," said the guard. He put his hands on his hips.

"Constable! Summon a constable!"

People stared at me. I was so embarrassed, I wanted to die.

"This isn't really me talking," I said to the people in back of me. "It's a little complicated to explain, but that wasn't the real me you heard just now."

They just stared at me. Then a uniformed policeman trotted up.

"What's the trouble here?" he asked.

"Oh, Constable, thank heavens you're here," I said in the Queen's voice. **"This ruffian refuses to let us enter the statue. We demand that he be severely punished."**

"You *demand* he be severely punished?" said the cop.

"Quite right," I said in the queen's voice.

"Oh, well, if you *demand* it, then I guess we have to follow your *orders*," he said.

"Exactly," I said in the queen's voice. But I think he was being sarcastic.

"And the reason I should follow your orders is that you're…?"

"The Queen of England."

"I see," he said. "The Queen of England. Well, I'm sure honored to be in your presence, Your Highness."

"Good," I said in the queen's voice.

"Let them in," the policeman told the guard. The people in back of us grumbled a lot, but there was nothing they could do. I think the cop let us in because he figured I was some crazy kid and he felt sorry for Dad. Anyway, we walked all the way up to the torch. Queen Victoria complained about all the stairs. But it was pretty cool at the top, I have to admit.

By the time we got back to Dad's apartment, I was so tired I could barely make it inside. Just then the phone rang. Dad answered it, talked for a while, then turned to me.

"Zack," he said, "you'll never guess who's calling."

"Who?" I asked. "Queen Elizabeth?"

"No, Great-Grandpa Maurice."

My Great-Grandpa Maurice, in case you didn't know, died and came back as a cat. He's living down in Florida and is looked after by a very nice lady named Bernice. We see him every once in a while. Last time was at a cat show at Madison Square Garden. We had asked for his help. The problem that time was that I'd been scratched by a weird cat and had started turning into a cat myself.

I took the phone.

"Hi, Maurice," I said.

"Zack!" said Maurice. "It's great to hear your voice! Not growing whiskers and a tail again, are you?" He laughed at his little joke.

"Nope," I said.

"Aww, too bad," he said. "We could've had a great time, lying in the sun and licking ourselves. So, what's new?"

"Not too much," I said. "Except Dad took me to a séance. And a ghost got inside me, and now she refuses to leave."

"Boy, I hate when that happens," said Maurice.

I could hear him take a long puff on his cigar and blow out the smoke. I've told him how dangerous smoking is. He laughs and says he's already dead, so what's the worst that could happen to him?

"Listen, bubbeleh," said Maurice.

"There's a big Inventors Convention at the Javits Center going on now. As you know, I'm quite an inventor myself. I'm bringing my latest gizmos to the convention. So come down and see me there."

"That's great!" I said. I was really glad Maurice was coming. If anybody could help me get rid of Queen Victoria, it was Maurice. "When are you coming?"

"Sunday," said Maurice. "Tomorrow."

"Cool!" I said. "By the way, what's your new invention?"

"A disposable diaper for puppies," he said. "I call it Poop-Doggy-Dog."

Chapter 7

The Javits Center is this huge glass building on the west side of Manhattan. It's not very tall, but it takes up maybe three square blocks. The Inventors Convention had already been going on a couple of days by the time we got there Sunday afternoon. And the place was a madhouse. There were about a million people there. They were all trying to sell their inventions. Wherever you looked, there were booths set up with the nuttiest inventions you could ever dream of.

"Hey, here's something you could use,"

said Dad. He pointed to a gadget that looked like a regular thermometer, only it had a kind of bulb on the end of it. It was called the Ya-Give-Me-Fever-Thermometer-Warmer. "It's for kids who want to fake sickness to stay home from school."

"That wouldn't work with *you*," I said. "Heck, you made me go to school once when I was *invisible*."

"Well, you weren't running a fever. And you know our rule about that."

We looked all over the place for Maurice. So far we didn't see him.

A red-haired woman wearing a shiny gold jump suit and large glasses with red frames came up to us.

"Howdy there," she said. "Would you like to see an invention of mine called The-Cat-Ate-My-Homework-Paper-Shredder?"

"You bet," I said. She showed us a flat metal box with rows of sharp teeth. "It turns any sheet of paper with writing on it into what looks like cat-chewed homework," she said proudly. "Packets of fake saliva sold separately."

We thanked her and walked on. Now we were in the pets section. I figured that was where Maurice's booth was located.

"Hello there," said a man with a wild look in his eye. He wore a red blazer, a polka-dot plastic bow tie, and a straw hat with a huge plastic dog bone on top of it. "Are you folks manufacturers?"

"No, we're not," I said. "Is this your invention here?"

"Not one but three," he said proudly. "First, we have the Barnum and Bailey Flea-Circus Dog Collar—for pet owners who are too soft-hearted to kill their pets' fleas."

"That's cool," I said.

"Have you ever had a goldfish that died?" he asked.

"Of course."

"Well, then you'll appreciate this. It's my Flush-a-Fish Funeral Kit—for toilet burials. It comes complete with a tiny water-soluble coffin, a cassette of organ music, and a short service for all religions."

"I like that," said Dad.

"And to avoid the problem altogether," said the guy with the plastic dog bone on his hat, "I've invented this." He held out a small orange plastic fish with a hinged tail. "Never-Say-Die Dave—the battery-powered goldfish you will *never* find floating belly-up at the top of your aquarium. Batteries not included."

That's when I spotted him.

"Dad, look!" I said. "There's Maurice!"

About ten yards away was a booth with a big yellow sign on top of it: POOP-DOGGY-DOG, THE FIRST DISPOSABLE DIAPER FOR PUPS! Sitting behind a table piled high with puppy diapers was a plump lady about the age

of my Grandma Leah—it was Bernice. And curled up in a basket on the table was the big gray cat who was my great-grandfather.

"Maurice!" I yelled.

The gray tomcat perked up his ears. Then he saw us.

"Dan! Zack, bubbeleh!" he called.

Dad and I rushed over to the booth. We kissed Bernice hello. I hugged Maurice and scratched him behind the ears.

"You guys look great," I said.

"So do *you* guys," said Maurice. "Did you bring your noodnick friend?"

"You mean Queen Victoria?" I said.

"Yeah," said Maurice. "Hey, Vicky, come on out and say hello!"

Queen Victoria didn't answer.

"Hey, Vicky, open a mouth and tell us something. What's the matter—cat got your tongue?"

Maurice cracked himself up over that.

"Sometimes she's very quiet," I said. "She might be sleeping."

"Sleeping! In the middle of the day? Only pussycats do that. Hey, Vicky, are you turning into a pussycat like me, or what?"

"We are most certainly *not* a pussycat. And our name is most certainly not *Vicky*. You may address us as Your Highness or Your Majesty, or you may not address us at all."

"Oh, come off it, Cookie. Drop the fancy-shmancy talk," said Maurice. "I bet we have a lot in common."

"Hmmph. What could we possibly have in common?"

"Well, for one thing, we're both old geezers who happen to be dead," said Maurice. "For another, I bet we know some of the same people."

"How absurd. A common alley cat and the Queen of England?"

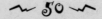

"Oh, I don't know," said Maurice casually. "What about a certain somebody by the name of...Prince Albert?"

"Prince Albert? *Which* Prince Albert?"

"Prince Albert of Saxe-Coburg," said Maurice.

"How dare you speak the name of my dear departed husband?" I said in the queen's voice.

"How I dare, doll face, is that Al and I are buddies. We hang out together all the time down in Florida. He was reincarnated as an English sheepdog."

"You're calling my sainted husband a dog? This is an outrage!"

"OK, Toots, you don't believe me, I can understand that. An old pussycat tells you your dead hubbie is now a sheepdog in Miami. I can see why you might not believe that. But what if I offered you proof?"

"**What sort of proof could you possibly offer?**"

"Proof. Well, let's see. Al introduced me to an old buddy of yours, Lord Melbourne. Your first prime minister? Your big buddy and advisor?"

"**I know who Lord Melbourne was.**"

"Yeah, well, Mel—that's what we call him, Mel—is now a hamster. Mel told me you hate anchovies."

"**You...you could have read that anywhere...**" I said in Victoria's voice. But there was something in her voice I had never heard before.

"I guess so," said Maurice. "But I doubt I could have read some of the personal things your husband, Al, told me. Like the pet name he had for you...*Poopsie-Pie.*"

I felt a sob catch in my throat. It was the weirdest feeling, because I wasn't sad. And then I started crying.

"I told old Al I was going to be talking to you this weekend," said Maurice gently. "He said, 'Be sure and give my love to Poopsie-Pie.'"

I started crying so hard I could hardly catch my breath.

Dad and Bernice looked really worried.

"Zack, what's the matter, son? Are you OK?" Dad asked.

Bernice handed me a handkerchief. I blew my nose into it big-time.

And then I just started babbling.

"Maurice...thank you for that message from my sweet husband, Albert...We are so sorry for doubting you...So sorry... We miss him so much...So very much..."

"Hey," he said, "don't worry about it, cutie. People doubt me all the time. Probably because of the cat suit. So, what brings you to New York?"

"We heard Madam Poopah was

holding a séance. We had some business here. And séances are good places to contact the living."

"What kind of business?" asked Maurice.

"It has to do with the new wax museum..."

"The wax museum?" said Dad. "What business do you have with the wax museum, Your Highness?"

"That wax dummy they have of me in the London museum. It looks so dreadful. So old and fat and frumpy. We wanted to make sure that the one in the new museum looked better. Younger. And...prettier. We're so sick of being thought of as a frumpy old queen."

A-ha! So, that was what was bothering Queen Victoria.

"We were young once, too, you know."

"So were we all," said Maurice. "You should have seen how cute I was as a youngster of sixty-five!"

"If only they could show us as a *young* Victoria. Alongside our beloved husband, Albert."

"Your Highness," said Dad, "I happen to know one of the people who runs the new Madame Chateau's Wax Museum. If you like, I could talk to him about that. I think he might like making you younger and prettier, with Albert by your side."

"Are you serious?"

"Of course," said Dad. "Tomorrow's Monday. I'll go and talk to him about it tomorrow."

"Oh, that would be marvelous! We thank you! We thank you from the bottom of our royal heart!"

"Your Highness," I said in my normal voice. "Now that my dad is going to get you

what you came to New York for, maybe you'd consider, uh...leaving my body?"

"Well..."

"Hey, doll," said Maurice, "how's about coming back down to Miami with us? I know a certain English Sheepdog who'd be mighty glad to see you."

"But how could we do that, Maurice?"

"Easy," said Maurice. "Why don't you just jump out of Zack's body and hop right into Bernice's?"

"Hey!" said Bernice. "Don't I have anything to say about who goes hopping into my body?"

"Of course, Bernice. You mind if Vicky hitches a ride to Miami inside you?"

Bernice sighed. "I guess not," she said.

"Great. So, Vicky," said Maurice, "how's about it? Want to go to Florida and meet a pooch I know?"

For a moment there was no answer.

Then, suddenly, a blinding flash of light and a huge puff of smoke. It felt like all the air was being sucked out of my lungs. I landed on the floor. Bernice was on the floor beside me. She looked confused and dizzy.

"Bernice, pussycat, you OK?" asked Maurice.

Bernice shook her head to clear it. Then...

"We would *love* to come with you to Florida," said Bernice in the Queen's voice. **"We cannot wait to see dear Albert again!"**

So, anyway, that's what happened. When the Inventors Convention was over, we all went out for high tea and scones. Then Bernice and Maurice hopped into a cab and went to the airport. I've never had to visit another ladies' rest room.

About a week later, Maurice called.

"Hey, Zack," he said, "how ya doing?"

"Great, thanks to you. It sure is nice not to have British old lady voices coming out of my mouth. How are you and Bernice?"

"Couldn't be better, kid. We sold Poop-Doggy-Dog to a pet supplies manufacturer in Detroit. Now we're trying to sell our new idea—Diapers for Pigeons."

"And what happened to Queen Victoria? Did she get together with Prince Albert?"

"Oh, yeah. That old English sheepdog was pretty happy about it, too. I found a vacant female Schnauzer who lived next door, and Vicky moved right into her."

Don't you just love happy endings?

What else happens to Zack?

Find out in

This Body's Not Big Enough for Both of Us

I had to go through the Count's bedroom to get to the bathroom. I looked around. Hmm. Right opposite the bed was a mini-bar. I wondered if there could be any Dr. Peppers in there. I opened the door and looked inside.

No candy. No Dr. Pepper. All there was inside the mini-bar were about twenty cans of tomato juice. They were labeled "Type B positive" and "Type A Negative." I took a closer look. Yikes! These were not cans of tomato juice. I was staring at twenty half pints of blood! I remembered the black candles and curtains and the black cloth over the mirror. Was Mella Bugosi a real vampire, like they said? If so, what were Spencer and I doing trapped in his hotel suite? And how could we get out of there before he decided to take a bite out of us?

THE ZACK FILES™

OUT-OF-THIS-WORLD FAN CLUB!

Looking for even more info on all the strange, otherworldly happenings going on in *The Zack Files*? Get the inside scoop by becoming a member of *The Zack Files* Out-Of-This-World Fan Club! Just send in the form below and we'll send you your *Zack Files* Out-Of-This-World Fan Club kit including an official fan club membership card, a really cool *Zack Files* magnet, and a newsletter featuring excerpts from Zack's upcoming paranormal adventures, supernatural news from around the world, puzzles, and more! And as a member you'll continue to receive the newsletter six times a year! The best part is—it's all free!

✂ ---